Jem and the Mystery Thief

Goldtown Beginnings Series

Jem Strikes Gold
Jem's Frog Fiasco
Jem and the Mystery Thief
Jem Digs Up Trouble
Jem and the Golden Reward
Jem's Wild Winter

Jem and the Mystery Thief

Susan K. Marlow

Illustrated by Okan Bülbül

Published by Kregel Publications, a division of Kregel Inc., 2450 Oak Industrial Dr. NE, Grand Rapids, MI 49505.

The persons and events portrayed in this work are the creations of the author, and any resemblance to persons living or dead is purely coincidental.

ISBN 978-0-8254-4627-6, print
ISBN 978-0-8254-7627-3, epub

Printed in the United States of America
21 22 23 24 25 26 27 28 29 / 5 4 3 2

Contents

New Words

aggie—a marble made from a stone called *agate*

aisle—a walkway

arithmetic—math

chum—friend

copybook—a book of blank or lined paper

gulch—a small valley

knucklebones—the game of jacks; played with a rubber ball and ten small objects

manzanita—a small evergreen tree with red bark, twisty branches, and berries that can be eaten

mischief—trouble

privy—a small outdoor bathroom; an outhouse
tart—a very small pie
thou—an old-fashioned word for "you"

CHAPTER 1

Countdown

Jem took a bite of his morning mush and made a face.

Not even pouring molasses on his hot cereal made it taste better.

He peeked under the table. His golden dog lay at his feet.

When Nugget saw Jem looking at him, his tail thumped.

"Good dog," Jem said.

Nugget could lick a bowl of mush clean in a hurry. Mama would never know.

But Jem's belly would know. It grumbled.

Jem was too hungry this morning to give Nugget his mush. He took another bite and made another face.

“Whatcha doing?” Jem’s little sister, Ellie, asked as she climbed up next to him on the split-log bench.

“Eating breakfast,” he said between mouthfuls.

Ellie pointed to a beat-up book. “No. What are you doing with *that*?”

“Nothing.” Jem slammed the book shut.

Paper was hard to come by in a gold camp. His school copybook cost five whole cents.

If Mama or Miss Cheney, the teacher, saw Jem wasting paper, there would be trouble.

Big trouble.

Ellie slumped. “Is it a secret?”

Jem shook his head. He looked around.

Mama was hanging clothes. They hung on a clothesline that was tied between two pine trees near the family’s big canvas tent.

Not far away, a pot of beans boiled on the outdoor cookstove.

“Hurry, Jem,” Mama called from her clothesline. “You don’t want to be late for school.”

Jem ate another spoonful of mush.

"If it's not a secret, then tell me." Ellie scooted closer. "Please?"

Jem put down his spoon. He might as well tell her. She'd pester him until he did.

"Oh, all right."

He opened his copybook to the last page. Five rows of crooked boxes took up the whole space.

Jem had written "May" at the top of the page.

"What is it?" Ellie asked.

"A calendar."

Ellie touched the first row with her finger. "Why are all those big Xs in the boxes?"

"Every morning, I cross out one more box."

"Why?"

Jem rolled his eyes. "Roasted rattlesnakes, Ellie! You ask too many questions."

Just then, Mama's words popped into Jem's head. *"Be patient with your sister."*

He let out a long breath. It was not easy being the big brother.

"I'm counting down the days until school is out." He slid his finger to the last day of May. "This box shows the last day of school."

"Yippee!" Ellie clapped her hands. "Then we play every day. Not just on Saturdays."

"Yep."

Jem liked playing with Ellie. Even if she talked too much.

Even if she tagged along behind him and asked questions all day long.

There was nobody else to play with. Not many children lived in Goldtown.

Only miners. A *lot* of miners. Maybe a thousand, or even more.

Some women lived in the gold camp too. Like Mama.

Jem sometimes wished he could play with his school chum Perry. But Perry's pa panned gold clear over in Two Bit Gulch.

The gulch was too far away to go visit a friend.

If he wanted to, Jem could go into town and play with Will Sterling.

He made a face. *Nope. Not mean Will.*

That rich boy always made fun of Jem and Ellie. He liked getting Jem into trouble, too.

Will's father owned the new gold mine up on Belle Hill. A lot of miners had stopped panning for gold in Cripple Creek. They worked for Mr. Sterling now.

The miners dug deep underground to find gold.

Pa said it was dark down there. And damp. And dangerous.

A shiver went down Jem's neck.

He hoped Pa never went to work for Mr. Sterling. He didn't want Pa to go down inside that deep, dark mine.

Ellie sighed. "I wish I could go to school."

Jem jerked his thoughts back to the breakfast table. "Huh?"

"I said I wish I could go to school."

"You want to sit in school all day?" Jem asked. "When you could be panning gold? Or catching frogs? Or playing with Nugget?"

"Mama won't let me go to the pond by myself," Ellie said.

Ellie was right about that.

"Panning for gold is hard work," she went on. "And the water is cold."

Right again.

"And Nugget likes you best." Ellie sighed again. "He even follows you to school."

Nugget's head popped up at his name. He crawled out from under the table. His tail wagged.

Jem didn't say anything.

"If I went to school, I wouldn't be so lonely all day," Ellie said in a small voice.

"Lonely?" Jem's eyebrows went up. "With Pa and Mama right here? And Strike-it-rich Sam and—"

"They're busy."

Ellie had a point.

Maybe school wasn't that bad. At least there was recess. And twenty kids to play with.

Jem looked at Ellie. Then he looked at Nugget.

Nugget was a good dog. He was friendly, and everybody liked him.

Everybody but mean Will.

It was also true that Nugget liked Jem best. The dog followed him everywhere.

Jem liked keeping Nugget nearby, but maybe . . .

He pushed away from the table. "I'll find a rope and tie Nugget up. That way he can't follow me to school. You can play with him all day."

"Really?" Ellie's eyes lit up.

"Yes, really!"

CHAPTER 2

Will Sterling

Jem slowed his steps when he walked into the schoolyard half an hour later.

"I wish I hadn't left Nugget home."

Ever since Nugget had become Jem's own dog, mean Will left Jem alone. He stayed far away from Jem and Ellie's pie wagon on Saturdays.

No more smashed pies. No more mean words.

Will didn't pick on Jem at school either.

Nugget followed Jem to school every day. He never barked. He no longer howled when the children sang.

Instead, Nugget plopped down under the big manzanita bush next to the schoolhouse. He rested in the shade and waited for recess.

During recess, the children played with Nugget.

Even Miss Cheney agreed that Nugget had grown into a very polite dog.

"Where's Nugget?" Jem's friend Cole asked. "Is he all right?"

The boys climbed the schoolhouse steps together.

"I left him home so Ellie could play with him," Jem said.

When he slid into his seat, two more children asked about Nugget.

Jem beamed. Everybody missed Nugget!

Everybody but Will.

"Dirty ol' dog," Will said in a low, mean voice.

He sat just across the aisle. His black hair hung over his forehead.

Jem's smile turned to a scowl. He wanted to say something mean to Will, but he didn't.

He kept his mouth shut tight.

The bell rang. *Clang, clang, clang!*

Jem looked at the empty spot next to him. Perry was not in school . . . again.

His friend was probably panning gold beside his pa. They panned in the creek that splashed through Two Bit Gulch.

Perry only came to school when it rained. Or if his mama made him go.

"Lucky duck." Jem put his chin in his hands and stared at his desktop.

Right now, he could be helping Pa and their prospector friend Strike.

Jem could be pouring water into the rocker box. Or panning gold beside Ellie.

A fist-sized gold nugget might wash into Jem's gold pan. Or maybe–

"Jeremiah Coulter."

Jem sat up straight. "Yes, ma'am?"

"Thank you for leaving your dog home," Miss Cheney said. "I was asked to take care of this problem."

Jem's mouth fell open. Nugget? A problem?

"There are to be no pets at school." The teacher sounded sad. "Please leave him home for the rest of the school year."

Jem nodded. He was too surprised to speak.

Will clapped a hand over his mouth. He choked back a laugh.

This is mean Will's fault, Jem thought.

For sure Will had told his father about Nugget. Mr. Sterling had told Miss Cheney.

Jem leaned across the aisle. "Tattletale," he whispered.

Will's cheeks turned red, but he didn't say a word. He just scowled at Jem.

The boys glared at each other until Miss Cheney rapped a ruler on her desk. "Let's begin our day."

Jem turned his head to the front. So did Will.

Miss Cheney read the Bible and said a long prayer. Then she put the Good Book away.

Will waved his hand in the air. "Miss Cheney! Miss Cheney!"

"What is it, William?"

He jumped up. "I have something special to show the class today."

Jem let out a big breath. *Roasted rattlesnakes! Not again.*

Will always had something to show the class.

One time he brought his Noah's ark. Each tiny wooden animal was hand-painted.

The ark's roof even came off. The animals fit inside the big boat.

Too bad Will didn't let anybody play with his precious Noah's ark.

Just last week, Will brought a five-pound chunk of gold ore to show the class. It came from the new mine.

"Father let me name our mine," Will had told the class. "I'm calling it the Midas mine. On account of rich King Midas in my storybook. Everything he touched turned to gold."

Jem wondered what show-off Will had brought today.

"Please come up here to share," Miss Cheney said.

"Yes, ma'am." Will walked to the front of the class.

"This is my coin collection." He lifted a leather pouch. It looked like Jem's gold pouch, only much bigger.

Will shook the pouch. Coins jingled.

Twenty children leaned over their desktops.

Jem leaned forward too. He wanted a better look.

Will opened the pouch and stuck his hand inside. "I have lots of pennies, dimes, and quarters, plus two five-dollar gold pieces."

He held up a big silver coin. "But this silver dollar is my favorite. See how shiny it is?"

No one said a word. Jem held his breath.

"You may come closer, children," Miss Cheney said.

The children sprang from their seats. They crowded around Will and his silver dollar.

"Ooh!" Clara said. "It's the prettiest thing I ever saw."

Everybody agreed.

Jem had never seen a silver dollar before. Not in all his seven-and-a-half years.

He reached out to touch the shiny coin.

"No!" Will knocked Jem's hand away. "You'll get it dirty."

Jem's cheeks grew hot.

Then something worse happened.

Will passed the silver dollar around to the big boys and girls. He also let everybody hold the gold pieces.

Everybody but Jem.

A big lump got stuck in Jem's throat. *Mean ol' Will!*

Miss Cheney didn't see Will's meanness. She was too busy looking at the coins.

Will finally returned to his seat. He dumped out the pouch and spread the coins on his desktop.

Miss Cheney's eyebrows went up. "What are you doing, William?"

“I want to look at my coins while I study my lessons,” Will said.

Will wasn’t the only one who wanted to look at the coins. The rest of the morning, Jem kept peeking across the aisle to see them.

He couldn’t help it.

CHAPTER 3

Silver Dollar

It was the longest morning of Jem's life.

His eyes would not stay on his arithmetic problems. Or on his spelling words.

He kept looking at the shiny coins on Will's desk.

Later, the sun shone in through an open window. The silver dollar sparkled even more.

Jem sighed. He knew why Will had knocked his hand away. Will was still mad because he couldn't pick on Jem and Ellie anymore.

Nugget wouldn't let him.

Miss Cheney finally told the class it was lunchtime.

Hurrah! Jem shot out of his seat. A whole hour to play!

Jem and the younger boys dashed out of the schoolhouse. They sat down under a tree and opened their tin lunch pails.

Jem ate the cornbread Mama had packed. He chewed on a stringy piece of jerky meat.

Then Jem saw the surprise. A blueberry tart.

Cole's eyes got big when he saw it. "I'll trade you two aggies for that tart, Jem."

"Nope." Jem smacked his lips. "My mama makes the best blueberry pies in Goldtown."

He ate his tart in four big bites. "Mmm." Crumbs dribbled down his chin.

Cole groaned. So did Michael and Owen.

"Let's play marbles," Will said just then. "I want to win my aggies back."

Jem shook his head. "I don't want to. I left my marbles inside."

He didn't want to play marbles with Will. Not after he wouldn't let Jem touch the silver dollar.

"Fair's fair, Jem," Cole said. "You have to give Will a chance to win his aggies back."

The other boys nodded. It was the rule.

"Oh, all right," Jem said. "I'll get my marbles. They're in my desk."

Jem ran across the schoolyard. He clomped up the wooden steps, into the classroom, and down the aisle.

He reached his hand inside his desk. Where was that marble pouch?

His fingers felt the soft leather. He yanked.

Out came Jem's marbles. Out came his copybook, two pencils, and six acorns. Out came his sling shot.

Jem stuffed everything back inside. Then he jumped up and spun around.

Thump! He bumped into Will's desk.

Will's coins went flying. Four dimes fell on the floor.

Jem sucked in a breath. *Uh-oh!*

Quick as a wink, he bent over and picked up the coins.

He dropped the dimes back on the pile. Then he looked around. No other coins had fallen off the desk. No coins had rolled away.

Good thing. He didn't want to lose Will's special coins. Not even if it was an accident.

Jem took one step toward the door. Then he stopped.

Will's shiny silver dollar lay only a few inches away.

Jem's fingers itched to hold that coin. His heart thumped against the inside of his chest.

I just want to hold it, he said to himself. *Just one time.*

What could it hurt?

Jem peeked around the room. Nobody was inside. The windows were wide open to let in the fresh air.

The windows also let in the schoolyard noises. Jem heard shouting and laughter.

Even Miss Cheney had gone outdoors on this sunny day. She was helping turn the jump rope for the girls.

Jem picked up the silver dollar before he changed his mind. "It's so heavy!"

He rubbed the coin between his fingers. "And so smooth. Shiny, too."

Even the gold Jem washed in his pan was not this shiny. "What a jim-dandy coin!"

"Hurry up, Jem!" Cole's voice sounded loud through the open window.

Jem nearly jumped a foot. His hand shook.

He dropped the silver dollar like it was on fire. It landed with a *clink* on top of the other coins.

Jem grabbed his marble pouch and ran out of the schoolhouse. He jumped off the porch.

"I'm coming!" he shouted. "Did you draw the circle?"

"Yes!" Cole yelled back.

A minute later, Jem crouched on the ground. He aimed his biggest marble. It was his best shooter.

Ready . . . aim . . . *fire*!

His marble smacked into Will's second-best aggie. Jem scooped it up and dropped it in his pouch.

Cole and Perry cheered and took their turns.

Will frowned. He dropped to his knees and went after the aggie Jem had won yesterday.

He missed.

Jem grinned but didn't say anything.

When Miss Cheney rang the bell, Jem

looked up in surprise. A whole hour could not have gone by so fast!

The boys picked up their marbles.

"Good game," Cole said.

"Good game," Jem said. His pouch clicked and rattled with three more of Will's special marbles.

Will didn't say, "Good game." He brushed the dust from his knees and said, "I'm going to win them back tomorrow, Jem. All of them. Every last marble."

Jem pulled the pouch strings tight. "Sure, Will."

"You can try," Cole said. "But everybody knows Jem's the best shot."

"I never shoot against Jem with *my* best marbles." Owen agreed. He laughed and took off toward the schoolhouse.

Jem ran to catch up. He plopped down in his seat and shoved the marble pouch into a corner of his desk.

Will slumped into his seat a minute later.

Jem didn't look at him. Pa said you never hit a man when he's down. Will had lost his marbles, and Jem would not rub it in.

Even if he wanted to.

Just then, Will jumped to his feet. He screamed at the top of his voice.

"My silver dollar! It's gone!"

CHAPTER 4

Missing Coin

Will's screechy voice sent the whole class crowding around his desk. The children all talked at once.

"What?"

"When?"

"Oh, no!"

"Children, please." Miss Cheney rapped her desk with a ruler. "Return to your seats and be quiet."

When nobody moved, she rapped louder. "Now!"

The children sat down. Everybody but Will.

A hush fell over the classroom.

"Are you sure it's missing, William?" Miss

Cheney asked. "Sit down and carefully look through your coins."

Will sat down and picked up a penny.

Jem propped an elbow on his desk. He rested his head in his hand and watched.

Will looked scared. His fingers shook as he dropped the coins, one by one, into the pouch.

He blinked. Two tears dripped down his cheeks.

Jem's eyes opened wide. Mean Will? Crying?

Will rubbed a sleeve across his wet face. "The coins aren't mine."

Jem sat up. The rest of the class gasped.

Miss Cheney's eyebrows went up. "What do you mean, William?"

"It's Father's coin collection. I saw the coin pouch on the desk in his office." Will sniffed. "I only borrowed it for today. I was going to put it right back after school."

Nobody said a word. Not even Miss Cheney.

A minute went by.

"It might have been best to keep your coins in the pouch," Miss Cheney said at last.

Too late now.

"Father will be so mad." Will gulped. "His specially minted silver dollar is missing."

A shiver went down Jem's neck. For once, he felt sorry for Will.

"Could it have fallen on the floor?" Miss Cheney asked.

Will didn't answer. He put his head in his arms on his desk and sobbed. His shoulders shook.

"Children." Miss Cheney clapped her hands. "We're going to help William find the missing silver dollar."

Everybody jumped up.

Everybody but Will. He kept his head down.

Cole double-checked inside the coin pouch. "Nope, it's not here."

Jem tapped Will's shoulder. "Maybe it's in your desk."

Will scooted over so Jem and Cole could reach inside the desk.

The boys pulled out five dead bugs, a crumpled piece of paper, two pen tips, and a crust of dried-up bread.

Jem made a face. *Yuck!*

But neither boy found the silver dollar.

Jem dropped to the floor. "Maybe it fell through a crack." He put his eye close to the floor and peeked into the space under the schoolhouse.

He couldn't see a thing. It was too dark.

"Look what I found!" Ruthie shouted.

Jem's head snapped up.

"My ring!" Miss Cheney clasped her hands together. "Thank you."

Ruthie dropped the ring into an empty teacup on Miss Cheney's desk.

More things soon joined the ring. Three buttons, the top from an ink well, five safety pins, and a hair clip.

But no silver dollar.

Miss Cheney laughed. "I didn't know our classroom was so untidy."

"Look here." Patrick, one of the big boys, held up a dead, wrinkly spider.

A *big* one.

Wes, another big boy, whistled. "That's a jim-dandy tarantula."

It sure was! Jem wished he had found it first.

Patrick held it higher. "Can I keep it?"

"Absolutely not." Miss Cheney pointed to the window. "Get rid of it."

Patrick's smiley face turned sad. But he did what he was told.

Miss Cheney ended the search. "Back to your seats, everyone."

Too bad, Jem thought. Looking for a lost coin was much more fun than doing lessons.

Everybody else must have thought so too. They moaned and groaned.

Will lifted his head. His face was red. His eyes were puffy.

He jumped up from his seat and clenched his fists. "I bet somebody stole my silver dollar!"

Will did not look scared or sad now. He looked angry.

"Shame on you, William Sterling," Miss Cheney scolded. "No one in our school would take another child's belongings."

"No, ma'am!" the children said together.

"My pa would warm my backside if I ever did such a low-down thing," Cole said.

Even the older boys looked shocked.

Miss Cheney glanced around the room. "We all leave our things lying out. Martha keeps her charm bracelet inside the classroom during recess."

"I don't want to get it dirty," Martha explained.

"But the coin's not here," Will said. "*Somebody* took it."

"William, that's enough," Miss Cheney said. "Besides, we were all outdoors during the noon hour."

Nobody said a word.

Will put his hands on his hips. "No, ma'am." He shook his head. "Somebody *did* go inside."

He pointed at Jem. "He did."

CHAPTER 5

Thief!

Miss Cheney's eyes got big. She wrinkled her eyebrows and looked at Jem.

"Is this true, Jeremiah?" she asked. "Did you go in the classroom during the noon hour?"

Jem nodded. "I had to get my marbles. They were in my desk."

"That's right, Miss Cheney," Cole said. "Will wanted to win his aggies back."

Jem swallowed. "I bet I'm not the only one who went inside. Lots of kids go in and out during recess."

"True." Miss Cheney looked around the room. "Please raise your hand if you came inside the classroom during the noon recess today."

No one raised a hand. No feet rustled. Nobody talked.

It was so quiet that Jem heard a squirrel chattering outside. A mockingbird sang. A crow cried *caw, caw*.

Jem could also hear his heart pounding in his ears.

Somebody must have gone indoors to put away their lunch pail. Or grab a ball. Or find another jump rope.

Maybe they were all too scared to answer.

"Did you see the coins on William's desk, Jeremiah?" Miss Cheney asked.

"Sure," Jem said. "He's been showing them off all morning. How could anybody miss them?"

The children laughed. Everybody knew Will was a show-off.

Miss Cheney rapped the ruler against her desk. "That will do."

The laughter stopped.

The teacher took a big breath and turned back to Jem. "Did you take the silver dollar?"

A lump got stuck in Jem's throat. It was hard to talk past the lump.

"No, Miss Cheney. I wouldn't do that."

Jem was learning the Ten Commandments in Sunday school. *"Thou shalt not steal"* was commandment number eight.

Will leaned across the aisle. "I bet you did," he whispered so only Jem could hear.

"I did not!" Jem shouted. His hands curled into tight fists.

"Jeremiah!"

Jem turned to Miss Cheney. His fists relaxed. "Yes, ma'am?"

"Did you touch any of the coins when you came indoors for your marbles?"

No, I didn't touch the coins was sitting on the tip of Jem's tongue.

Just then, commandment number nine popped into his head. *"Thou shalt not bear false witness."*

Mr. Bates, Jem's Sunday school teacher, had told his class that "Thou shalt not bear false witness" was another way of saying, "Don't lie."

Jem knew all the commandments. Bible verses were easy to learn.

Mama said it was amazing how the Good Book stuck in Jem's head.

Pa said the easy part was learning the

verses. The hard part was doing what the verses said.

Pa was sure right about that.

Jem didn't want to answer Miss Cheney. He couldn't. His tongue was stuck to the roof of his mouth.

"Did you touch the coins?" the teacher asked again.

Commandment number nine spun around inside Jem's head. *Don't lie. Don't lie. Don't—*

"Answer me this instant, Jeremiah," Miss Cheney said in a growly voice.

Jem's tongue got unstuck in a hurry. "Yes, ma'am. I touched Will's silver dollar but—"

The children gasped.

Cole's mouth dropped open. "Jem!"

Jem's hands felt slippery with sweat. This day was turning terrible.

"Children!" The ruler rapped again.

"I didn't take the silver dollar." Jem's eyes stung. "I just wanted to feel how heavy it was. I put it right back."

"You did too take it," Will said. "You're a thief."

"I am not!" Jem jumped up. "Don't call me that."

He grabbed Will's shirt. He yanked him out of his seat.

Then Jem pushed Will down hard and sat on him.

"Ow!" Will hollered. "Get off me!" He wiggled, but he was stuck.

Jem held Will down.

"I didn't take your silver dollar," Jem said in a shaky voice. "If I wanted to steal a coin, I would have picked the five-dollar gold piece. It's worth a lot more."

A firm hand came down on Jem's shoulder just then. Another hand took his arm.

"For shame, Jeremiah Coulter." Miss Cheney pulled Jem off Will. "Go stand in the corner," she said, pointing.

Scary shivers raced down Jem's neck. The corner?

The one at the front of the classroom? The one where everybody could see him?

He looked up into Miss Cheney's face.

The teacher's cheeks were red. She looked angry.

No wonder. Jem had broken a school rule. *No fighting.*

"Obey me at once," Miss Cheney ordered.

"But—"

"Go. Now."

Jem snapped his jaw shut before he broke another school rule. *No talking back.*

He hurried to the corner before Miss Cheney could yell at him some more.

CHAPTER 6

The Corner

Jem stood in the corner for the rest of the afternoon.

He knew everybody was looking at him. His face felt hot.

He should not have sat on Will.

Jem sighed, but only to himself. Miss Cheney didn't want to hear any noise from the corner.

Jem's legs grew tired. He rested one leg. Then he rested the other.

His eyes grew tired too.

There was nothing to look at but the big corner crack. It ran from the high ceiling all the way down to the floor.

The crack was where the two walls came

together. Only, they didn't come together very well.

Just then, something wiggled out from the crack.

Jem perked up. What could it be? He looked closer.

A big black spider crawled out. It crept up the wall.

Jem tipped his head back and watched it climb higher and higher.

A minute later the spider came down and crawled back inside the crack.

Jem leaned closer to the corner. Maybe the spider would–

"Good-bye, Miss Cheney!"

"Good-bye, children."

Shouts and laughter told Jem that school was over for the day.

He stood still and waited for Miss Cheney to tell him he could go home.

She didn't.

Jem bit his lip and stared at the crack.

The minutes dragged by. Miss Cheney's heels went *click, click, click* as she crossed the room.

Why doesn't she let me go home? Jem asked himself.

He knew better than to say those words out loud.

Miss Cheney cleaned the blackboard. Her eraser made rubbing noises.

Jem didn't peek. Instead, he watched a

fly walk around on the wall. It walked closer and closer to the big crack.

Maybe the spider would jump out and grab the fly. That would sure be something to see!

"Come out, spider," Jem whispered. "There's a fly at your door."

Miss Cheney's heels clicked again. She walked down the aisle, away from Jem. The clicking sound went away.

The teacher was gone for a long time. Where did she go?

A new voice told Jem the answer.

"Jeremiah."

Jem forgot about the spider. He forgot about the fly. He spun around.

Pa was walking toward him. His shirt was dark with sweat. Dried mud covered his pants and boots.

Uh-oh. Somebody had pulled Pa away from his gold panning.

Click, click, click. Miss Cheney marched up the aisle behind Pa.

No wonder the teacher had not let Jem go home. She was waiting for Pa.

Pa held out his hand. "Come along, son."

Jem left the corner and took Pa's hand. His stomach felt like a tight knot.

Was he in big trouble?

Jem and Pa walked out of the schoolhouse and down the steps.

"Good-bye, Mr. Coulter," Miss Cheney called from the doorway.

Pa looked behind his shoulder. "Good-bye, Miss Cheney."

Halfway home, Pa squeezed Jem's hand. "I got an earful from Miss Cheney when I got to school."

He smiled. "Now, why don't you tell me what happened?"

The knot in Jem's stomach melted.

Pa was a good listener. Jem told him everything.

He told him how he had sat on Will.

He told him how he remembered to obey commandment number nine. "Even if I didn't want to at first."

Pa gave Jem's hand another squeeze. It felt good. "I'm proud of you for telling the truth."

"I'm going to catch the real thief," Jem said. "No matter how long it takes."

"That's a good idea," Pa agreed. "Until the real thief is found, people will keep thinking you did it."

"I know."

"A good name is rather to be chosen than great riches," Pa said. "That's what the Bible says."

Jem nodded. "That's why I'm going to find the thief. I want a good name."

When they got home, Pa went back to the creek.

Ellie ran up to Jem. "A big boy came and got Pa," she said. "Are you in bad trouble?"

Jem shook his head. "I don't think so."

He looked around. Mama was taking down the clean clothes. She didn't look mad. She looked tired.

"I'm *glad* you sat on Will," Ellie said. She giggled.

"Roasted rattlesnakes!" Jem yelped. "Did that boy tell Pa and Mama everything?"

Ellie nodded. "Yep." Then her eyes lit up. "Maybe Will's the thief. Maybe he took his own silver dollar."

Jem rolled his eyes. "Why would he do that?"

"To get you in trouble."

Jem thought about Will. He thought about the silver dollar.

Then he shook his head. "No, Ellie. Will looked scared. The silver dollar is really missing."

He clenched his fists. "I'm going to catch that thief. I *have* to."

CHAPTER 7

More Mischief

Jem didn't go to the creek that afternoon. He didn't pan for gold. He didn't play with Ellie.

He was too busy thinking about how he would catch the thief.

Nugget ran out from behind the tent. He barked and raced to Jem. He wagged his tail and licked Jem's hand.

Nugget missed Jem. He wanted to play.

Jem cheered up when Nugget brought him a stick. Jem threw the stick and chased his dog.

Soon, he and Nugget were sitting next to the creek.

Ellie waded out of the water and plopped

down beside her brother. Her beat-up pie pan hit the ground with a *clang.*

"Panning gold is hard work," she said.

Jem threw a rock in the water. "So is catching a thief."

"If you didn't take Will's silver dollar, then who did?" Ellie asked. "Who else went inside?"

"Nobody."

"Somebody must have," Ellie said.

Ellie was right. Maybe the thief wasn't telling the truth when Miss Cheney asked them to raise their hands.

Jem thought hard. Who else might have gone inside during recess? Cole?

No, Cole had played marbles the whole time. So had Will and Owen.

What about one of the older boys? Wes Morris?

No. Wes and the big boys had played with Wes's dirty-gray donkey. It always bucked and kicked.

It looked like fun to ride a bucking donkey, but Jem never asked. He stayed away from Wes and Patrick and their friends.

A new thought made Jem's heart thump. One time when he looked at the donkey, Wes was not there. Maybe he had sneaked inside!

Jem shivered. Could a little boy tattle to the teacher on a big boy? No.

He hoped the thief was somebody else.

* ★★★ *

The next day, Jem played marbles during recess. He kept one eye on the game. He kept his other eye on the schoolhouse.

It was not a good idea.

Will won back two of his aggies. "You're playing sloppy today, Jem." He laughed.

Will was right about that.

It was tricky to play marbles and watch the schoolhouse at the same time.

"What did your pa say about the missing silver dollar?" Cole asked Will.

Will's laughing face turned scared. "I didn't tell him. Father hasn't missed it yet."

"Lucky for you," Owen said.

The bell rang just then. Noon recess was over.

Jem picked up his marbles in a huff. Not one person had gone inside! Not even Miss Cheney.

Catching a sneaky thief was hard work.

Jem had just sat down at his desk when Martha started crying.

"My charm bracelet is gone," she sobbed. "I took it off, like I do every day." She pointed to a small bottle of ink on her desk. "I left it right here by my inkwell."

She wiped her eyes and glared at Jem.

Jem's face turned hot.

His face grew even hotter when Miss Cheney looked in her teacup. "The ring Ruthie found yesterday is missing too!"

She shot up from her chair. "Children, I don't know what is going on, but this must stop."

Her angry voice made shivers run up and down Jem's arms. Especially when she looked at him.

"Did you go inside during the noon recess, Jeremiah?"

"No, ma'am!"

Jem had stayed outdoors on purpose. Going inside was not a good way to clear his name.

Miss Cheney didn't let the children search the room today. "I am sorry about your bracelet," she told Martha. "Let's hope it turns up."

Martha slumped in her seat.

Miss Cheney faced the class. "Begin your lessons."

Jem opened his spelling book, but he didn't think about spelling. He thought about the thief.

Who had stolen Martha's charm bracelet? Who would want that clunky, jingly ol' thing?

Not me!

Jem was sure nobody had gone inside.

But . . . wait!

Wes and the big boys had taken the gray donkey behind the schoolhouse. They were gone for most of the noon hour.

A new thought jumped into Jem's head. *The schoolhouse has two doors!*

Jem had only watched the front door. He'd forgotten all about the back door.

He peeked over the top of his spelling book.

Three big boys sat near the back wall. Wes was the oldest. He was in the seventh grade and was almost as big as Pa.

Wes and his family had come to Goldtown two months ago. Pa called them a "rough bunch."

That was a nice way of saying the new miners were mean and bossy.

Jem was scared of rough Wes. He never asked to ride Wes's donkey. He knew the big boy would say no.

Wes saw Jem looking at him and made a face.

Jem spun around. His heart pounded. He stared at his spelling words.

Maybe Wes had sneaked inside and stolen Martha's charm bracelet.

And Miss Cheney's ring.

And Will's silver dollar.

Jem hoped not. He did not want to tattle on Wes.

He also knew he would have to watch the schoolhouse a lot better if he wanted to catch this mystery thief.

CHAPTER 8

Jem's Excellent Idea

It rained on Friday.

Only a few boys went outside for the noon recess. The rest of the children stayed indoors.

Miss Cheney closed the windows and lit a fire in the stove.

The boys played checkers or did word games on the blackboard.

The girls played knucklebones with a ball and ten small stones.

Jem didn't play. He walked behind the teacher's desk. A door opened into a small room.

There wasn't much inside.

A broom, a mop, and a pail sat in a corner. Miss Cheney's coat hung on a hook.

Jem opened the back door and looked outside. It would be easy to sneak inside from here.

He would have to watch both doors. But how?

All the way home that day, Jem thought about the two doors.

"I can't watch the back door and the front door at the same time!" he yelled at the rain.

He stomped in a mud puddle. Water splashed up. Mud splattered his pants.

Jem would have to think of a different plan.

"If I peek through a window, I can see everybody who goes inside." He stomped in another puddle. "I wouldn't have to watch the doors. I could see the whole room."

What a jim-dandy idea!

* ★ ★ ★ *

On Saturday, Jem told Ellie about his plan.

She put down her gold pan and looked at him. "That's a good idea, but—"

"But what?"

"You'll have to hide in the bushes," Ellie said. "You don't want the thief to see you spying on him."

Jem nodded. "There's a manzanita bush near a window. It's where Nugget always stayed. I can hide there."

Ellie was not done talking. Like always.

"What if there's nothing good left in the classroom for the thief to take?"

Jem groaned. He would never clear his name.

Not if the thief stopped taking things.

He thought and thought. Then he snapped his fingers. "I'll find something worth lots of money. I'll put it on my desk-top so the thief can see it."

Ellie wrinkled her eyebrows. "Like what?"

Good question.

What did Jem have that was worth money? His gold pouch?

Nah. The thief would think the pouch held his marbles. Marbles were not worth much.

Then Jem got an idea. An *excellent* idea.

He jumped up. "I'll be right back!"

Nugget barked and ran after Jem.

Jem ran along the creek bank. It was only raining a little.

Not far away, Pa and Strike-it-rich Sam were pouring dirt and water into the rocker box.

"Pa!" Jem yelled so that Pa could hear him. The rocker box was noisy. "Can I borrow your pocket watch?"

Strike stopped pulling on the handle. Pa stopped dumping water and dirt into the box.

"Why?" Pa asked.

"Your watch would make good bait, like fishing. Only, I want to catch a thief."

Strike laughed. "Seems like an expensive way to go about it, young'un."

Pa agreed. "I'm sorry, Jem. I can't let you borrow my watch."

Jem sighed. Then he got another idea. "Come on, Nugget!" They raced away.

A minute later, Jem stopped in front of the tent. "Mama!"

Mama pushed aside the tent flap and hurried outside. "My goodness! What's wrong?"

"Can I borrow your special locket?"

"*May* I," Mama said, smiling. "Why do you need it?"

Jem talked fast. He told her about his great idea.

Mama sat down on a tree stump. She lifted Jem onto her lap and gave him a hug.

"You're an honest boy," she said. "Pa and

I know you didn't take Will's coin. Or any of the other missing items. I'm glad you want to catch the thief, but maybe you should forget about this. School will soon be out."

Jem slumped. Mama and Pa and Ellie believed him. But what about Miss Cheney? Or the other kids?

He had to clear his name.

"A good name is rather to be chosen than great riches," Jem said in a small voice.

Mama squeezed Jem tighter. "I'm sorry, but my locket is too precious. Pa gave it to me on our wedding day. I can't take the chance that it might be stolen."

Jem nodded and slid off Mama's lap. She sounded sad.

Jem felt sadder. What now?

He called Nugget and went back to the creek.

Ellie was washing gold. Dirt, rocks, and sand swirled in her pan.

Most of it fell out.

"Slow down," Jem said. "You're going to lose all your gold."

Ellie giggled. "I'll just pick it up and try again."

Jem rolled his eyes. Little sisters could be so silly.

He scooped three handfuls of gravel and sand into his gold pan. He dipped it in the water.

"Did you think of something to put on your desktop?" Ellie asked. "So you can catch the thief?"

Jem shook his pan back and forth. "No."

Then a new idea popped into his head. "Do you want to help me catch the thief?"

"Yes!" Ellie's eyes lit up.

"Then let me borrow your necklace. The one you got for Christmas."

Ellie sucked in a big breath. "My silver necklace? No!"

"I'll take care of it," Jem said. "I promise. I have to catch that thief."

Ellie shook her head.

Jem thought some more. "What if I rent it from you?"

"What does that mean?" Ellie asked, frowning.

"It means I'll pay you one pinch of gold dust every day to let me borrow your locket."

Ellie wrinkled her forehead.

Jem knew she was thinking hard. "Well? How about it?"

"All right," Ellie said. "But *two* pinches a day."

Jem let out a big breath. *Sisters!*

He set down his gold pan and held out his hand. "It's a deal."

CHAPTER 9

Sneaky Thief

Jem walked to school on Monday in a downpour. Rain was not nice to Goldtown miners.

Squish, squish, squish. Mud sucked at Jem's boots.

By the time he climbed the steps and found his seat, mud speckled his pants from ankle to knee.

The rest of the children had muddy feet and legs too. Even Will.

Jem sniffed and wrinkled his nose. What a stink!

The classroom smelled like wet hair and damp, dirty clothes.

He felt inside his pocket. Ellie's necklace was safe. He kept it hidden all morning.

"Thank goodness the rain has stopped," Miss Cheney said when the clock showed twelve o'clock. "Outside, all of you."

Jem pulled Ellie's necklace from his pocket and laid it carefully on his desktop. Then he hurried outside.

It was too muddy to play marbles, so the boys played tag.

All except Jem. He headed for the privy. It was the only idea he could think of to get away.

Nobody would miss Jem if they thought he was in the privy.

He ran around the back of the school, past the privy, and clear around to the other side. He ducked behind the manzanita bush that grew near one of the windows.

Even if the children chased each other around the schoolhouse, they would not see Jem. The manzanita was too bushy.

Jem grabbed the high window ledge. He pulled himself up on his tiptoes and peeked inside.

The classroom was empty. Ellie's necklace lay on his desktop.

"Come on, thief," Jem whispered. "Come inside and take Ellie's necklace."

Just then Jem heard a noise. Was the thief coming? Was it . . . Wes?

"I hope not." He held his breath and watched.

Two girls skipped inside, but they didn't stay long. They put away their lunch pails and skipped out.

Nobody else came inside the classroom. Not Wes. Not Cole. Not Will.

Not even Miss Cheney.

Jem watched through the dirty window until his fingers got tired. They slipped.

Down he went.

The bell rang. No thief today.

Jem shook his head and went back to class.

* ★ ★ ★ *

Two more days passed. The rain stopped for good.

The California sun shone bright and hot. It dried up the schoolyard mud in a hurry.

Halfway through the morning, Miss Cheney called to Patrick and Wes. "Please open all the windows."

She wrinkled her nose. “It stinks like a miner’s tent in here.”

The children laughed. They knew what a miner’s tent smelled like.

The boys opened the windows.

A warm breeze blew through the classroom. It blew the stinky smell right out.

At noon the sun shone even hotter. The marbles came out. So did the jump ropes.

The children raced outside.

For the third day in a row, Jem pulled Ellie’s necklace from his pocket.

“Renting you is costing me a fortune,” he told the necklace. “Two pinches of gold a day. My worst idea ever.”

His pouch would soon run out of gold dust.

He laid Ellie’s sparkly necklace on his desktop. “This is the last day. Then I’ll do what Mama says and forget about the whole thing.”

Even if he never cleared his name.

Jem pounded down the schoolhouse steps. He ran around the corner and slipped behind the manzanita bush.

Then he pulled himself up on his tiptoes and looked through the open window.

The sun was shining. It shone through the window on Ellie's necklace.

It sure is pretty, Jem thought. *A real prize for a thief.*

He watched and waited, but no thief came into the classroom.

Nobody came in. It was too nice outside.

Then the worst happened. "Jem, where are you?"

Uh-oh! Somebody missed him. It was time to go back.

Rustle, rustle.

Jem froze. What was that? It was close by, right near the other window.

Slowly, he turned his head. Something big and black settled on the window ledge.

It was a crow. The biggest crow Jem had ever seen.

He sucked in his breath and held it.

The crow hopped through the open window and landed on Miss Cheney's desk. It poked its beak into her teacup.

Jem's eyes opened wide in surprise. He held tighter to the window ledge. His fingers hurt.

Jem didn't make a sound. He didn't move. He kept holding his breath.

What was that crow up to?

The shiny black bird took another big hop and landed on Jem's desk. It walked around, looking at Ellie's necklace.

The crow cocked its head toward Jem. Its beady black eye blinked.

Jem couldn't hold his breath much longer. His fingers started to slip.

Quick as a striking snake, the crow picked up Ellie's necklace with its beak. It hopped back to Miss Cheney's desk, hopped up on the windowsill, and flew away.

Just like that.

CHAPTER 10

A Good Name

Jem's breath came out in a big *whoosh.* He didn't waste a second.

He let go of the window ledge, dropped to the ground, and crawled out from behind the manzanita bush.

He shaded his eyes. The crow was flying high and far.

"No!" he yelled at the crow. A big knot tied up his belly.

Jem had planned to catch a human thief. Somebody he could knock down and sit on. Or somebody he could tell the teacher about.

That way he could get Ellie's necklace back.

But a crow? This was terrible! How did a boy catch a thief that could fly away?

"Ellie will cry and cry when she finds out I lost her necklace for good."

Jem's feet took off. He could not let the crow get away.

Even if it meant breaking another rule. *Don't leave the schoolyard.*

"Miss Cheney will make me stand in the corner again," Jem said. "But I don't care."

He stopped, panting. Where did that thief of a crow go? He looked up.

A large hawk circled high in the sky. Four little birds swooped and ducked.

No crow.

Jem looked toward the middle of town. There it was!

The big black bird was hard to miss. It was flying lower now.

"Drop that necklace, you thief!" Jem yelled.

He didn't care about the silver dollar. He didn't care about Martha's charm bracelet.

He didn't even care anymore about clearing his name.

He just wanted to get Ellie's necklace back.

The crow ignored Jem and kept flying.

Jem ran faster. He crossed two dirt streets. Then—

Jem tripped over a big rock and fell on his face. *Ow!*

He jumped up and kept his eyes on the crow.

The crow flew into the branches of a big oak tree.

Breathing hard, Jem waited. When the bird didn't come out, Jem waited some more.

Finally, the crow flew away.

Jem dashed to the oak tree. It was easy to climb. Higher and higher he went.

Where was the crow's nest? "Please help me find it, God," he prayed.

A minute later, Jem spotted the crow's huge nest. He pulled himself up on a branch that hung over the nest.

He looked down and gasped.

The nest was full of treasures. Ellie's necklace. Lots of rings and pen tips. Martha's charm bracelet. And—

Will's silver dollar!

Jem also saw earrings, a silver spoon, three marbles, and dozens of shiny buttons.

The schoolhouse was not the only place this thief had robbed.

Jem reached into the nest. He stuffed the silver dollar, Ellie's necklace, and Martha's charm bracelet into his pockets.

He would come back later for the other treasures.

Quick as a wink, he climbed down the tree.

Jem thought hard all the way back to school. This crow had been stealing things for a long time.

But why had the crow only started stealing from the classroom the past few weeks?

The answer came like lightning. Nugget!

Nugget always stayed under the manzanita bush. When Jem stopped bringing his dog to school, the crow was free to fly in and out of the open windows.

Jem laughed. He had caught the thief.

Will would get his silver dollar back. Martha would get her charm bracelet back.

And Ellie would get her necklace back.

Best of all, Jem would clear his name.

"A good name is rather to be chosen than great riches," Jem said as he clomped up the steps.

He burst into the classroom.

Miss Cheney put her hands on her hips. "Jeremiah Coulter, where have you—"

"I caught the thief!" Jem shouted. He emptied his pockets onto Miss Cheney's desk. "And you won't believe who it is!"

A Peek into the Past: The Mystery Thief

Do crows really take shiny objects back to their nests?

Most people who study crows say no. Others insist crows *do* collect shiny objects.

Jem and the Mystery Thief is based on a true story that happened over eighty years ago. A fourth-grade teacher and her pupils could not figure out how items from their portable classroom went missing.

The children kept watch. They soon discovered a crow was flying through the window when everyone went out to recess. They followed the crow and found its nest, just like Jem did.

Not long ago, a young girl in Seattle, Washington, liked to feed crows in her backyard. The crows began to leave small gifts in return. The girl now has a collection that includes a silver bell, buttons, Lego bricks, a blue paper clip, a piece of foam, a heart from a necklace, and dozens of other items.

Crows are smart. They can solve problems. If they meet a "mean" person, they teach other crows to stay away. They don't forget a person's face.

Some crows drop nuts on the road and wait for a car to crack them open. The crows are not run over by traffic. Why not? Crows know what the traffic light means. They wait until the light turns red before putting their nuts down. They fly off when the light turns green. Then the crows wait for the next red light to pick up their nutty treats!

* * ★ * *

Download free coloring pages and learning activities at GoldtownAdventures.com.